MARVEL

Fantastic Four
A FAMILY ANTIMATTER

Written by
Stacy McAnulty

Illustrated by
Matt Kaufenberg

MARVEL

Los Angeles • New York

They've conquered villains, destroyed monsters, and halted disasters. They are . . .

the Fantastic Four–

the **world's greatest** super hero team.

Thanks to them, Earth is currently safe and, according to some . . . less exciting.

"I'm so bored," Johnny complains.

This is **Johnny Storm**–the **Human Torch**. He can fly, and he runs a little hot.

"I once handled baddies," Johnny says.

"Now you handle the s'mores, and you do an excellent job," their loyal robot H.E.R.B.I.E. replies.

Sue Storm, Johnny's brilliant older sister, is the **Invisible Woman**. Not only can she disappear, she can create force fields, which is helpful on rainy days.

Ben Grimm is the **Thing**— an ace pilot and the strongest man on Earth.

He can clobber villains and lend a hand by taking out the trash.

And finally, the genius scientist **Dr. Reed Richards** is **Mister Fantastic**. His ability to stretch and change shape makes him nearly indestructible.

He's *fantastic* at keeping everyone safe, even kittens.

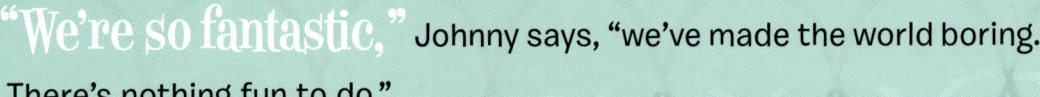

"**We're so fantastic,**" Johnny says, "we've made the world boring. There's nothing fun to do."

"We could play checkers," H.E.R.B.I.E. offers.

Johnny rolls his eyes and heads to the Baxter Building lab instead. "I wonder what the others are up to."

Reed is happy to explain.

...EINSTEIN—
ROSEN BRIDGE...
HYPOTHETICAL...
ALTERNATE UNIVERSE...
ELECTRONS...
POSITRONS...
ANNIHILATION...

Johnny understands about three of the words Reed uses, so Sue simplifies: "We're trying to open a wormhole."

"Wormhole!" Johnny understands that word. "Those can take us anywhere in space and time, right? We can relive our greatest battles."

Johnny may have found a solution to his boredom.

That night, Reed and Sue must attend the Empire State University awards dinner. They ask Johnny to join them, hoping to keep him busy and, more importantly, away from their lab.

"I'd rather eat an earwax Popsicle," Johnny answers.

Sue instructs H.E.R.B.I.E. and the Thing to keep an eye on Johnny.

But the moment they leave . . .

Johnny fiddles with controls—controls he should not be fiddling with—and a **wormhole** to a Cretaceous world opens.

"Mr. Johnny, I must demand you stop at once!" H.E.R.B.I.E. says.

"Sure," he says. "After I wrestle this *T. rex* with his puny arms."

Thankfully, the wormhole collapses before they become dino chow. So Johnny opens another.

"This is better than a museum," Johnny says.

But again, the wormhole closes too quickly.

Johnny continues to play with the dials, hoping to *dial up* one of their great battles, like when they fought the Mole Man or Namor.

But before he can find an epic replay, the Thing barges into the lab.

"Johnny! You are NOT supposed to be in here!" he shouts.

The outburst startles Johnny, who accidentally turns a knob too far.

A dangerous **wormhole** rips open!

"Watch out!" Johnny yells.
"It's the Negative Zone!"

It's too late. H.E.R.B.I.E. is sucked inside.

"Hold open the wormhole!" Johnny tells the Thing. "I'm going after H.E.R.B.I.E.!"

"Be careful, Mr. Johnny," H.E.R.B.I.E. warns. "The Negative Zone is a dangerous parallel universe of antimatter."

"And that matters because . . . ?" the Human Torch asks.

"You are made of matter. I am made of matter. Everything we know is made of matter. And when matter meets antimatter, it's **instant annihilation**," H.E.R.B.I.E. explains.

"You could have told me this before I followed you in," the Human Torch says.

Back in the lab, the Thing struggles to keep the wormhole open. He calls for reinforcements. *Literally.*

"Reed! Sue! Help!"

"We need to get them out of there," Sue says.

However, returning from the Negative Zone is impossible.

"There's only one way out," Reed explains. "And that is to never go in."

"Now is not the time for riddles, Reed," the Thing says.

Exactly! They need to hurry. H.E.R.B.I.E. is hurtling closer and closer to the vortex—a point of unspeakable power, a point of no return.

"Mr. Johnny, save yourself. This appears to be my demise," H.E.R.B.I.E. says. "My circuits are freezing up. I . . . I . . ."

"No way. No one freezes on my watch," the Human Torch replies.

"Flame on!"

The Human Torch reaches H.E.R.B.I.E., but when he tries to turn back, it's useless. The pull of the vortex is **too strong**.

"I got the robot," the Human Torch tells the others. "Now would be a good time to demonstrate our teamwork skills. **Get us out of here!**"

The Human Torch is right. **They must work together.**

"On our way." **Mister Fantastic** stretches from one universe into the other.

While the **Invisible Woman** creates an antimatter force field.

And the **Thing** keeps them anchored to their world.

"There!" Mister Fantastic spots the Human Torch and H.E.R.B.I.E.

The Invisible Woman wraps them in a protective force field.

"Gotcha! You are in so much trouble, Johnny!"

"Don't you think I'm too old for a time-out, sis?" the Human Torch says.

"Quit the arguing. The wormhole is **collapsing**," the Thing warns.

"Heading home now," Mister Fantastic replies. "We just need two more minutes."

The Thing groans, "You've got **one**, and that's being generous by about fifty seconds."

They're not going to make it!

"We need to move faster," Mister Fantastic says. "We need **more energy!**"

"That's it!" the Invisible Woman exclaims. "We're surrounded by antimatter, and when antimatter and matter meet—"

"Instant annihilation!" Johnny says, proudly showing off his new science knowledge.

"Yes. It creates pure energy." The Invisible Woman yanks off her necklace. "An explosive force we can ride home. Brace yourselves."

She launches the necklace and . . .

BOOM!

They **blast** through the **Negative Zone** and exit the wormhole moments before it collapses.

"That was **exhausting**," the Thing says.

"That was **twenty-seven seconds**," Mister Fantastic says.

"That was **too close**," the Invisible Woman says.

"That was **fantastic!** Total opposite of boring," the Human Torch says.

"That's the **last time** I'm watching Mr. Johnny. Please don't ask me again," H.E.R.B.I.E. begs.

"The Fantastic Four save the day once again," Johnny says. It turns out that boredom is no match for the world's greatest super hero family.

"Can you just stick to s'mores, Johnny?" the Thing asks.

"Sure. At least for tonight," Johnny replies. "Who knows what might *open up* tomorrow."

The World of Fantastic Four

H.E.R.B.I.E.

Humanoid Experimental Robot B-Type Integrated Electronics is a robot created by Reed to assist the Fantastic Four around the Baxter Building and on their adventures (and to occasionally keep an eye on Johnny).

Mister Fantastic

Dr. Reed Richards is a brilliant scientist and engineer; some consider him the smartest man in the world. Like all the members of the Fantastic Four, he obtained his powers after being exposed to cosmic radiation during a space mission. Mister Fantastic can stretch and take nearly any shape, making him almost indestructible. Reed is Susan Storm's husband.

The Invisible Woman

Susan Storm is also a genius and works side by side with Dr. Richards in their laboratory in the Baxter Building. After the cosmic ray exposure, she gained the ability to turn invisible and create protective force fields. The Invisible Woman can also make other objects invisible. Sue is Johnny's older sister and Reed's wife.

The Negative Zone

The Negative Zone is a dangerous, parallel universe to our own. In this alternate space, everything consists of antimatter. (Compare this to our known universe, which is primarily made up of matter.) For the most part, the Negative Zone is a void, but a few villains have lurked here. Exiting the Negative Zone is nearly impossible.

The Human Torch

Johnny Storm has a thirst for adventure and prefers to speed through life in fast cars and airplanes. As the Human Torch, he turns to fiery plasma, giving him the ability to control fire and also fly. Johnny is Sue's younger brother.

The Thing

Ben Grimm is an ace fighter pilot who became the Thing after their life-changing space mission. He has super-strength and is nearly invincible. His bulk does not make him slow or clumsy. Unlike the others who appear human and control their powers (turning them off and on), Ben is always the Thing and never looks human. Ben is Reed's longtime best friend.

Protons and neutrons

Matter Atom

Electrons

Atoms

These teeny-tiny particles are the building blocks of all matter. In the center of an *atom* are protons and neutrons; orbiting them are electrons, which have a negative charge. (Think of magnets. One side is positive, and one side is negative.) Types of atoms include hydrogen, helium, and oxygen. When atoms bond, they make molecules.

Matter

Matter is anything that takes up space and has weight. That can be something huge and heavy (like a freight train) or something so small that a high-powered microscope is needed to see it (like a single blood cell). Nearly everything in our universe is made of matter, including you. And matter is made of atoms.

Positrons

Antimatter Atom

Antiprotons and antineutrons

Antimatter

Antimatter is considered the opposite of matter. That's because instead of being made of atoms with electrons and protons, antimatter has positrons and antiprotons. When antimatter and matter meet, it is beyond explosive. The matter and the antimatter are destroyed (annihilated!), creating a massive amount of energy. There is very, very little antimatter in our universe. So don't worry about accidentally bumping into any.

Wormholes

A *wormhole* is a theoretical tunnel from one point in space and time to another. No wormholes have ever been created or discovered; they are only *considered* possible. If a wormhole did open, it would likely be unstable and dangerous. Scientists are excited about wormholes because they would offer humans shortcuts through space. Instead of taking 200,000 years to travel across the Milky Way, it would be like stepping through a doorway. Another name for a wormhole is an Einstein-Rosen bridge.

Light Speed

This is the speed limit for our universe. Nothing can travel faster than the speed of light (186,000 miles per second). Because space is so vast, traveling from one side of the Milky Way galaxy to the other at *light speed* would take 200,000 years. That's why scientists are interested in finding or creating wormholes—they could be shortcuts across space and time.

Some science!

For my Fantastic Fam:
Cora, Lily, Brett, and Henry –SM

For my Fantastic Five:
Emily, James, David, Daniel, and Henry –MK

First Edition, June 2025
10 9 8 7 6 5 4 3 2 1
FAC-034274-25100
Printed in the United States of America

This book is set in Burbank Small, Ed Roman, and Ed Script
Designed by Emily Fisher

Library of Congress Control Number: 2024946327
ISBN 978-1-368-11402-8
Reinforced binding

Visit www.DisneyBooks.com and Marvel.com